FRIENDS
OF ACPL

W9-BAZ-693

A CRITERION BOOK
FOR YOUNG PEOPLE

Falter Tom
and
The Water Boy

Falter Tom
and
The Water Boy

by MAURICE DUGGAN

Illustrated by KENNETH ROWELL

CRITERION BOOKS   NEW YORK

© 1958 BY MAURICE DUGGAN
LIBRARY OF CONGRESS CATALOG CARD NUMBER: 59-12200

A slightly different version of this book is
published in England by Faber and Faber, Ltd.

PRINTED IN THE UNITED STATES OF AMERICA

For

NICKY

CO. SCHOOLS

C482945

PUBLISHER'S NOTE

This story originally appeared in the School Journal, Department of Education, New Zealand, to whom acknowledgement is made

FALTER TOM AND THE WATER BOY

Falter Tom was old. He had been given his nickname because of his stiff leg which gave a peculiar style to his walk. At one stride he would seem to be setting off on some far journey; at the next, drawing his stiff leg up to his good leg, he would falter and frown, pause, and stride out again. The look on his face matched his walk. When he was striding out, his face was bright and his eye was lively; when he faltered, his face became angry and sad. Falter and frown, stride and smile; so he went along.

If he had another name it had been long forgotten. It might even have been forgotten by Falter Tom himself. Once, many years ago, someone had come to the town inquiring for a Mr. Thomas Kevin O'Hennessy; but no one had heard of such a man and no one thought it could be Falter Tom. So the man went away. And whether it was Falter Tom or not, who could say?

Falter Tom once told the postmaster that he was eighty-four years of age. "And fifty or more of those years were at sea," Falter Tom said. "Where I got my game pin, you should know, striking at whales. A good deal south of here, I don't mind telling, and in colder water."

But he looked too young to be eighty-four. His eyes were too bright, his tongue too quick. The postmaster looked at him and wrote down, on the form he was filling out, *Falter Tom: aged seventy-one years.*

Why seventy-one and not seventy? Because the postmaster was a man who thought all round figures looked too much like a guess.

From his brogue you would know that Falter Tom was Irish; though you wouldn't be able to tell just what part of Ireland he was from, north, south, east, or west. And from his talk you would know him for a sailor: he talked all day of ships and the

sea. He wore, in all weathers, dark whipcord trousers, and a tight buttoned jacket. In summer he never wore less; in winter he never wore more, except an old peaked cap faded and turned

8

almost green with time. On the tip of his chin he had a white tuft of hair, much like a goat's beard except that it was trim and spotless. From his upper lip, curling down over the corners of his mouth, hung a moustache; it was as white as the foam on a wave and it shone like silk. He was proud of his whiskers. His fingers touched them, and stroked and curled them, ruffled and smoothed and tugged at them. His eyebrows might have been drawn on to his brown face with a white crayon. Altogether he was a man you would look at twice.

Of sea stories Falter Tom had a hundred which he expected you to believe; and two hundred which, whether he expected it or not, you could never quite believe. Those who heard them, those two hundred stories of pirates and treasure and sea-monsters, of freak storms and mutiny and shipwreck, smiled as they listened; smiled with enjoyment but couldn't quite believe them. Except, of course, for the very youngest boys in the town who swallowed down his stories, with their mouths as wide in wonder as any stranded fish, and their eyes as large in amazement as any bicycle lamp. They would stare and gasp. Falter Tom would tell them a salty tale, wink at them, then shoo them off as though they were tame birds. When next he saw them he would tell them the same story back to front and upside down: but whichever way he told it, the story was as wonderful. He didn't, however, want them to believe too much.

"You might find wonders as great as that," he would say. "Find them any morning on your way to school, if you'd but keep your eyes about you."

But the young wondering boys looked in vain for shipwreck and mutiny in Potter's field; searched in vain for treasure under the piles and planks of Mill Road Bridge; watched in vain for mermen and freak storms on the calm surface of Komata Creek. Nor was there any secret chart hidden in the bit of a hollow in the plane tree by the school gate. They shot their stick guns into the wild tiger branches of the pines along the road; but had you asked them they would have said that they didn't believe Falter Tom at all.

Falter Tom's favourite walk was along the shell road that turned out over the promontory, the headland that made one arm of the bay. He faltered out of the town's one main street at nine o'clock every morning, wet or wind, sun or cloud. He liked it most when the sea was running, and the great slow waves struck on the rocks, and the plumes and feathers of spray came curling and blowing up over the low cliff. Falter Tom loved, he said, the salt on his lip. He would stand half-sheltered behind the battered old fig tree and peer from under his peaked cap, giving a wise commanding stare to the sea. You could find him there any morning; until the day he disappeared. And when he did disappear the stories told of him were very strange indeed; stranger than any of the two hundred strange stories he himself told. But he knew a lot about the ceaseless sea; anyone would have agreed with you about that.

One morning, at about ten o'clock on a mill-pond day, Falter Tom climbed slowly down the steps cut into the cliff; down to a patch of sand, no bigger than an asparagus bed, uncovered by the tide. The sand was hard. Falter Tom crossed it, half a stride at a time, and got himself on to a rock which the sun had dried. He sat down and took out his pipe. He was just bringing the burning match up to the bowl of the pipe when he saw something moving, swimming and rolling in the shallows out beyond

the slow wash at the sea's edge. He put his pipe away, unlit, and climbed off the rock for a closer look.

"It's likely a dolphin, in for the warm water," Falter Tom said to the mild air. "At this time of the year it's what you'd expect."

He crossed the sand until his shining boot toes were almost at the water's edge.

"Fish," he called, "are you enjoying your swim?" He saw it swimming and rolling. "Haven't I met you somewhere, maybe?" Falter Tom called. "Off the coast was it? Or out to sea it could have been."

He chuckled to himself at his little joke. He was just reaching for his pipe again when he saw that it wasn't a fish at all. It lay still on the surface of the sea and he saw that it was a boy, and an odd sort of boy at that. It had skin that was as green as a leaf, and hair as long as a pony's mane and as copper-coloured as a new penny. It was watching him, Falter Tom saw.

"Sonny," Falter Tom called. "What game are you up to? It's a dangerous place for a boy to be swimming. What gear, ever, have you on? Is it fancy-dress, or what? You'd best come out before the tide gets you. Come on now. Come out."

He thought he knew what it was. It was a boy in one of those new-fangled diving outfits, a sort of bright rubber helmet; and the green was his bathing suit. But he wasn't sure. There was something odd about it.

"Do you hear me?" he shouted. "Be pleased to come out when I say. I'm Falter Tom. You'll know me. And you'll know that when it comes to the sea I know what I'm talking of. It's no place for a boy to be swimming. Be so good as to come out."

The boy rolled over, seemed to listen, and swam away as fast as a fish. He rolled at rest on the sea, farther away from Falter

Tom than ever; though not far enough away to be out of reach of his voice or the glance of his eye.

"Do you not understand you might drown?" Falter Tom called. "I'm too old to be rescuing you. You might drown, I say."

A bubbling watery laugh came back to him. There was a splash, a flick of green, and the boy was gone. Falter Tom stood still and stared. He pushed back his old cap and shaded his eyes with his hand.

"He's likely playing jokes," Falter Tom said to himself. "He doesn't understand the sea."

Falter Tom was staring at the spot where the boy had disappeared when the bubbling laugh rose again from somewhere near his feet. There lay the green boy with copper-coloured hair, staring up at him from the shallows. He was no ordinary boy at all, Falter Tom saw. He wore no underwater diving suit: his skin was green, and his eyes were as slanted as a cat's eyes, and as merry as Christmas.

"Bless me, boy," Falter Tom said. "What manner of thing are you ever? I thought you were having a prank with me. Are you fish or merman, or what?"

"I thought a sailor would know," the boy said. "I'm a water boy."

"Aah," Falter Tom said, touched on his pride of knowing the sea. "Now I was wondering could you be that. I've not met you before, have I? I don't remember your like. But if you know me for a sailor, perhaps you'll know my name?"

"Of course," the water boy said. "Falter Tom. I've been watching you for weeks while you have been watching the sea. It's not an ordinary name, is it?"

Falter Tom was growing quite used to the strange appearance of the boy. He even began to think him rather handsome in an odd sort of way. "It's a nickname," Falter Tom said. "I've a bit of a limp, do you see?"

"Nickname?" the boy said. "What is that?"

"Well, a sort of friendly title," Falter Tom said. "Haven't you such a thing yourself?"

"I've had no need of it," the boy said, "until now."

"Then we must make something up for you. Something with the sea in it. I'll give my mind to it."

"Will you be here tomorrow?" the boy asked.

"Indeed," Falter Tom said, "if you've been watching me you'll know I never miss a day."

"You thought I was a fish," the boy said.

"An honourable mistake," Falter Tom said. "I see now that you're not. I've always been a man to believe my eyes."

"If you tell no one that you saw me, I'll be here tomorrow," the boy said. "I'll meet you. Good-bye."

The water boy stood up, waist deep in the water, and walked out to sea until his head disappeared under a wave. He was gone. "Now swither me," Falter Tom said saltily, staring with surprise. "Except that I do believe my eyes I'd swear I was dreaming. I'll tell no one, that's sure. Who is there who would believe me?"

Next morning the wind was up and the sea was running. Falter Tom climbed down on to the sand and stood in the salt spray. He was pleased to feel it on his face. He hadn't been there long when he caught sight of the water boy rolling like a porpoise in a wave that broke, as Falter Tom watched, and surfed the boy inshore.

"Good morning," the water boy called. His voice was piping, shrill and clear though not very loud. "It's rough on top," he said.

"Aye," Falter Tom said. "Do you live in the sea, or what?"

"I'm not to come out of it," the water boy said. "I'd drown."

"Come," Falter Tom said. "Drown in the air? On dry land? You're making fun of me."

"Indeed I am not," the boy said seriously. "I'm a water boy. I told you that at half-tide, yesterday."

"You did," Falter Tom said. "And I beg your pardon for forgetting it."

"Will you come in, then?" the boy asked.

"Me?" Falter Tom said. "Is it into the water you mean? I'd drown for sure. I'm no swimmer and I'm too old to learn. You must excuse me."

"You won't drown," the water boy said. "I promise you that."

"It's too big a promise," Falter Tom said. "I don't see how you could keep it. I'm a mite too heavy for a boy to keep me afloat. You'd never do it. And I'm too fond of life to risk it."

"Look," the boy said. "Will you put your foot in, then?"

"Well, I might. But I don't see the use of it. I know what the sea feels like. And then I'd have to take off my boot and roll my britches."

"No," the boy said. "Will you put your foot in as it is? Boot and all, I mean? You'll see why I ask."

Falter Tom looked down at his shiny boots. He polished them each morning and he didn't like the idea of plunging even one in the sea. "It would be folly," he said. "It would rot it."

"Then I must go," the boy said, and turned back to the breaking water.

"Just a minute," Falter Tom called. "I'll do it; though it's a daft enough thing for anyone to do. But if I have to, I will. So long as you'll stay. So long as you'll remember the favour."

"Put your foot in," the boy said. "Then count to twenty and take it out."

Falter Tom looked at the boy's green, bright, handsome face, and took a step across the shelf of rock and plunged his foot and leg into the sea. The sea didn't feel cold; indeed Falter Tom couldn't feel anything.

"One, two, three . . ." Falter Tom counted. And at twenty he drew his foot out and stepped back on to the dry sand. "There," he said. "Now I've obliged you."

"Look at your boot," the boy cried, laughing, and turned and walked quickly back under the sea.

"Here, I say," Falter Tom called. "Come back. That's hardly fair, to go off like that when I've been decent enough to oblige you."

"Tomorrow," the bubbling, faint voice cried back.

Falter Tom looked at his boot and the leg of his whipcord trousers; the boot was shining still; his sock and trouser leg were as dry as a biscuit. He moved his toes; they felt dry and comfortable.

"Well I'm swithered," he said. "What's happening to me ever?" He bent down stiffly and plunged his hand in the sea and drew it out; it was wet and the water dripped from his fingers. " 'Tis a trick of some sort," he said, and looked down again, in wonder, at his dry and shining boot.

Falter Tom hurried through the town on the following morning, faltering as fast as he could go. He could hardly wait, in his excitement, for his slow, lame leg to catch up. In front of the post office he stumbled, and growled at himself, frowning, looking angry.

"Falter Tom," the postmaster called. "You mustn't rush things so. You're trying to do too much. The sea will wait. Remember you're eighty-four."

"Impudence," Falter Tom muttered, too quietly for the postmaster to hear. "I'm not a day over seventy-one." But he did not stop: he waved to the postmaster and went on. There wasn't time to waste in talking.

The water boy was waiting. Falter Tom filled his pipe and walked out on to a shelf of rock. The tide was as far out as it could go. At this time tomorrow he wouldn't be able to stand on the rock without getting wet.

"Boy," Falter Tom said. "I'd give a lot to know your secret. The water didn't touch me at all. Dry as a bone I was."

"Will you come in now?" the boy said. "You won't get wet. You saw what I can do."

"Ah, that's another thing you're asking," Falter Tom said. "A boot's one thing, even a leg. But the whole of me, dry in the wet sea—that's something different entirely."

"You don't trust me," the boy said.

"Now don't say that," Falter Tom said. "I do, as far as I'm able. But you might be taking on more than you can manage. Have you, for instance, done such a thing before?"

"I've never spoken to anyone else," the boy said, lying as lightly on the sea as a boy on a rubber float. "It was only when I'd seen you so often that I thought I might speak."

"Indeed, you did wisely," Falter Tom said. "All right," he said, a moment later. "I'll try it. What can I get but a wetting?

17

And I've had that before, more than once. And the sun is out, so I shan't chill. Though I'm not used to being led by a bit of a boy —no offence, mind. I'm an old dog to be learning new tricks. But what do I do?"

"Nothing at all," the boy said, excited now that Falter Tom had made up his mind. "Just walk into the sea."

"I'll look an old fool should anyone be watching," Falter Tom said. "But then I'll not much mind that."

"You'll have to put your pipe out," the boy said. "It's hard for me to manage so that you can keep that alight in the sea."

"I should never have dreamed it to be possible at all," Falter Tom said. "I'd best leave it on the rock with my tobacco and matches."

"There's no need," the boy said. "They'll be safe in your pocket."

Falter Tom and the Water Boy

Falter Tom came slowly back along the ledge of rock and stepped down to the sea. The water boy lay, waiting and smiling, lifting and falling in the waves. Falter Tom put away his pipe, looked up once at the blue sky as if asking it to forgive him for being so foolish, so simple an old man, and faltered steadily out into the short choppy waves without so much as one glance down at his boots or his clothes. The water boy coasted inshore and lay on the water just ahead of him, keeping just out of reach as Falter Tom advanced. When Falter Tom was standing up to his neck in the water, the boy stopped him.

"Shall I count to twenty?" Falter Tom asked.

"There's no need," the boy said. "You're safe now."

Falter Tom raised an arm above the water and looked at it: it was dry. It was unbelievable that it should be so. He turned and looked inshore to the beach, the breaking waves, the cliffs, and the steps of the track. It was more unbelievable still that he should be looking back at them as he stood up to his neck in the salt sea. He was glad no one was watching. They would have thought him very mad indeed.

"I'd never have dreamed this could happen to me," Falter Tom said. "Not at my age."

"Are you old?" the boy asked, softly. "Are you, do you think, as old as I am?"

"Boy," Falter Tom said, "your eyes will give you the answer to that."

"Can you remember a time before there were people on that land, there? Before there were ships?"

"I'm not pretending to be that old," Falter Tom said.

"How old are you?" the water boy said. "Though it's rude, perhaps, to ask."

Falter Tom was just about to answer, eighty-four, when something stopped him. "I'll tell you the truth," he said. "I'm seventy-one years of age; and six months and some days more. So you see, you are a bit of a boy still."

"I can remember languages no one speaks now," the boy said. "And ships no one sails. I can remember tribes and peoples who live no longer on the old shores. I cannot tell how old I am. I seem always to have been in the sea."

Falter Tom gave a shout of laughter and swallowed the top off a wave. The boy was so serious about it that it was more amusing than if he had smiled while telling it. Falter Tom loved a tall story himself. He coughed and choked and shouted with laughter again.

"That's harder," the boy said.

"What?" Falter Tom said. "What's that? What's harder?"

"To breathe in the sea," the boy said naturally, smiling at Falter Tom's amused face.

"Oh, I can breathe," Falter Tom said. "So long as I've my head free I'm comfortable enough."

"That's not what I meant," the boy said. "Watch."

The water boy turned and flipped under the sea. His copper-coloured mane of hair was the last of him to disappear. Falter Tom looked down his nose and saw the boy standing on the sandy bottom, his head just level with Falter Tom's waist. The boy stayed under five minutes or more and Falter Tom watched. Then the boy let himself float up to the surface and he broke through the water just by Falter Tom's beard. He wasn't even puffing.

"Of course it's easy for me," the boy said. "That doesn't really prove anything, I suppose."

"What was it you intended to prove?" Falter Tom said. "I'm afraid I don't understand."

"Why, that you can do it too. You don't think I meant you just to stand there up to your chin in the sea. It wouldn't be kind."

Falter Tom licked at another wave as though it had been an ice-cream cone. He was very surprised. "Now, boy," he said. "I'll admit you're very obliging. And you'll admit, I hope, that it's not everyone who would have taken you at your word. But if you are about to suggest that I put my head under water and hold it there, I'm afraid I must say no. I couldn't do it."

"No," the boy said, frowning, thinking. "That wouldn't work. I'll think of something."

"Don't," Falter Tom said. "Don't bother yourself. We've come far enough for one day. The tide's turned. I can feel it."

"There's no hurry," the boy said. "We've lots of time."

"I'm glad to hear you say it. But I think I'd best be getting along in."

Falter Tom reached down through the sea and took out his old round heavy watch and looked at it, before he remembered that it, too, had been all the time in the sea. He peered at it carefully and held it to his ear. The water boy watched him. The watch ticked clearly and told the time boldly.

"I have it," the boy said. "You must find the charm. And you must bring it tomorrow, no later than an hour after daybreak. And you must not drink anything or eat anything, or talk to anyone, after midnight."

"Sonny," Falter Tom said softly. "I'm an old man. I live on my pension. I've none of your charms or whatever they are. I'm a simple fellow."

"Part of a fish and a piece of gold kept all for luck. That's the charm," the boy said. "You must find it."

"There's little hope of it," Falter Tom said. "I've nothing that would do."

"You must find something," the boy said. "You must."

Falter Tom thought: the water came up to his chin and he took an easy step or two backwards until his head was clear again. He felt quite as though he were standing on dry land, except that in the sea it was much more like lying down. The water supported him. "I've nothing," he said. "Nothing that will do. But what's it all for? You must tell me that."

"So you can breathe," the boy said, as if it were the simplest answer in the world. "There are things I want to show you, under the sea."

"Now swither me, boy," Falter Tom said. "Am I not in far enough? I don't know that I'm game for much more."

"Trust me," the boy said. "Have you come to harm? Do you feel cold or tired with standing in the sea?"

"No, I don't. To be honest, it's an improvement on leaning against that old fig tree up there."

"Is there nothing you could bring?" the boy asked. "Won't you go home and search, and come back tomorrow with whatever you find that will do? I'll be here. Part of a fish and a piece of gold kept all for luck; that's the charm. And nothing to eat or drink, nor any word to anyone, after midnight."

"I hold out no hope of finding such a thing," Falter Tom said. "But I'll look. I can do that, at least."

"Splendid," the boy cried, his voice as shrill as a calling bird. "And be here no later than an hour after daybreak. I'll be waiting. But you must go in now."

22

Falter Tom and the Water Boy

Falter Tom wanted to ask a hundred questions, but there was no time. He walked quite quickly out of the sea and waved in reply to the boy's green, waving arm.

"It's a wonder," Falter Tom said. "There's no other way of putting it." He examined his watch again, his pipe and tobacco and matches. He was as dry as he had ever been and the match burst into flame when he struck it on the box. "It's a wonder," he repeated, as he climbed up from the beach. "But I'm not so loony that I'll believe him to be more than twelve. Part of a fish and a piece of gold was what he said. Kept all for luck. Now there's a riddle." He put his feet carefully into each step of the rock path and climbed up, one step at a time. "But the rest is easy enough. Nothing to eat or drink, and no word to be spoken, after midnight. And I'm an early riser from my sailoring days, so I'll be there in time. But the charm; I've no idea of that."

On his faltering way home Falter Tom stopped at the post office. "Postmaster," he said, "I've to confess I've been spinning you a yarn, and I'm sorry, though I meant no mischief. I'm seventy-one years old; and six months and some days more. That's the truth of it, and you've a right to be angry if you want."

The postmaster didn't mind at all. He was very pleased to find that his guess had been such a good one. Now if I'd put down seventy years on that form, he thought, I'd have been wrong. It would have been a round number, and I'd have been wrong. "Excellent," he said to Falter Tom. "Fine. I guessed it, you see, to the year. Seventy-one you say? Excellent." He patted Falter Tom's arm and walked with him to the door of the post office. "You must look after yourself, Falter Tom," he said. "You've been rushing things lately. What is all the hurry for? What is there out at the point that you must get there in such a hurry?"

"At the point?" Falter Tom said, pretending surprise. "Well, there's the sea. But I know of nothing else. Nothing. I like the salt on my lip, as you know, but that's the whole of it."

Falter Tom went down the two steps from the post office and stood in the road. I'll have to be a bit more careful, he thought. What would the boy say if I brought the whole town out with me one morning? I'd likely never see him again.

"I'll walk out with you one day," the postmaster said. "I'm fond of the sea, too, in my way. Though there's no time for it when you've a job to do, as I have. But stop by for me, some-time, and I'll get my wife to keep an eye on the place for an hour or two, and we'll stroll to the sea."

"Aye," Falter Tom said. "We must, some day." But he didn't mean it. He began to walk away when he remembered the charm he must find. He stopped, then turned back to the post office.

"Postmaster," he said, "I was reading a bit of a thing the other day, in a magazine. About a sort of lucky charm some man had to find. A fancy tale it was, but it set me wondering. The charm had to be part of a fish and a piece of gold; something kept for luck. Now what would a thing like that be, ever?"

"Umm. I've not the slightest idea," the postmaster said. "It sounds a peculiar sort of story. Didn't it say?"

"No," Tom said. "It didn't."

"Don't worry your head over it," the postmaster said. "It doesn't sound important. I'm too busy for riddles, I'm afraid. Good-bye." And he went back into his office.

"Not important," Falter Tom muttered. "That's all he knows."

He walked off towards his house, a white cabin with a white

shell path and a walnut tree. His walk was slower: he thought the postmaster might be watching him out of his window. He let himself into his tiny house and put on the kettle and made himself a cup of tea. He sat over his tea, thinking. After a little while he fell asleep.

When he woke it was almost dark. "What am I thinking of?" he cried. "I've no time to be sleeping. I've the charm to look for." He got up and lit the oil lamp and in its light he searched the walls and shelves of his cabin-cottage trying to find something that would fit the boy's words. There was nothing. He took a key from a peg on the wall and crossed to the window and opened the old sea chest covered with a rug which he used as a couch. It was filled with a sailor's duffle, oilskins, and bits of sail canvas, sail needles, queer shells and stones, an old map or two, an old brass quadrant used in navigation, photographs of himself as a whaling sailor, but nothing that would do. He put the things one by one on the floor until the box was empty. "Nothing," he said aloud. "Nothing that would do."

He knelt by the empty chest. He raised the lamp and put it on the window-sill. As the light moved something caught his eye; something shone for a second in the corner of the chest. Falter Tom reached down, curious and quick. At first his fingers found nothing, but then he drew from the leather lining a length of gold chain. The chain had hanging from it a whale's tooth set in gold. He'd forgotten it and he looked at it in surprise. "I wore it on my Sunday waistcoat," he said. "It's thought by some people to be lucky, and I suppose I believed it then." He held it in his hand and it shone in the light. "Part of a fish and a piece of gold kept all for luck," he shouted to the empty room. "That's it! A whale's tooth on a gold chain. I've found something."

He was very pleased. He tumbled the things back into the chest, slammed down the lid, and carried the lamp and the chain to the table. "The only thing is, a whale isn't a fish," he said. "But perhaps it won't matter. I've nothing better. And a whale swims in the sea. It will have to do." In his excitement he drank a cup of stone-cold tea and didn't even notice. "I'll know in the morning," he said. "People would say I was crazy to be thinking of such things, and yet I do trust the green lad, for all his jokes."

Next morning Falter Tom woke before daylight. He went out into the dark cool yard at the back of his house and pumped a bucket full of water from the well. He stood the bucket on the lip of the well and plunged his head in as deep as he could get it. He stood up, gasping at the coldness of the water, and scrubbed at his hair and his whiskers.

"It will be cold in the sea, at this hour," he said to himself. "But no. You don't feel it when you're with the boy."

He tipped the dregs of water over the roots of a blue hydrangea. He went inside, dried himself, and put a kettle of water on the stove. There was water at the taps, but Falter Tom liked to wake himself of a morning with water from the cold, clear well. It reminded him of his sailoring days.

He made himself a cup of tea and sat down by the window, on the old chest, to drink and to watch the last star fade and day begin to grow. When his tea was cool he took a long drink. He swallowed a mouthful before he remembered what he was doing. He jumped up, as quick as a cricket, and knocked the cup to the floor. "Now swither me," he said. "I'm a forgetful old man. I clean forgot."

He stood by the window, puzzling out the best way to put things to right again. "I swallowed no more than a spoonful," he said at last. "It will maybe never be noticed. I'll not remark on it." He put the whale-tooth and chain in his pocket, picked up the broken cup and put it on the sink, and went out of the door, along the shell path, under the walnut tree, and walked towards the point and the sea. Half-way along the one street of the town he met the milkman out on his early round.

" Morning, Falter," the milkman said. "You're about early. Will we get a fine day do you think?"

Falter Tom remembered, just in time, that he was not to speak to anyone that morning. He shut his lips tight and nodded at the milkman and waved his hand, and faltered off as fast as he could.

"Now that's not like Falter Tom," the milkman said, watching him go. "He must have something on his mind. It's very odd."

Falter Tom hurried to the sea. At the foot of the cliff the tide was not quite full, but the little bit of beach was almost covered. He climbed down the steps to where the boy was waiting, floating on the sea, singing a watery, bubbling song that floated to Falter Tom over the water, like a breath of sea air, a little flurry of singing wind.

"Have you brought it?" the boy called, stopping his song. "Have you found a charm? And have you done all the things I said?"

"Aye," Falter Tom said. "I've something that will do, I think."

"What is it?" the water boy asked, swimming in closer.

"A whale's tooth mounted in gold; on a gold chain."

"A whale's tooth?"

"It's not a fish, I know," Falter Tom said. "But will it not do as well?"

"It's marvellous," the boy said, springing up and down in a shower of spray. "It's out of the sea."

"I used to wear it for luck," Falter Tom said.

"Splendid," the boy cried and he looked very glad. "But first we have to be sure that everything is all right, before we begin. Will you put your foot in the sea again, please? And count twenty, as you did before? Will you do that?"

"Indeed," Falter Tom said, "I will. I have the habit of it now."

He plunged his foot in the sea and counted twenty and pulled it out. The boot and sock and trouser leg were wringing wet.

"Oh," the boy wailed. "It's all gone wrong. What have you done? You haven't told me the truth. You haven't done as I asked?"

Falter Tom looked at his wet boot. "It's my own fault entirely," he said. "I should have told you. I didn't eat anything, and I found the charm, and it's all true about that; and I didn't talk to a soul. But I made myself a cup of tea. . . ."

"You drank something?" the boy said.

"A spoonful, only," Falter Tom said. "I remembered it too late."

"It won't work now," the boy said. "We will have to try again. We have only tomorrow left. If it doesn't work then it won't work at all. I will have to go now and explain that you didn't mean it, because if they thought you were just telling a lie they wouldn't let me do it, ever."

Falter Tom was pulling off his boot and sock. "Who are *they*?" he said. "What have *they* to do with it?"

The water boy shook his head. "You are not to know," he said. "But remember, tomorrow; nothing to eat and nothing to drink and no word to anyone, after midnight. And bring the charm to me not later than an hour after daybreak. I can't stay now. They are a long way off."

The green water boy vanished with his copper-coloured mane into the sea. Falter Tom waited a little while for the sun to dry out his sock and then faltered slowly back through the town, down the shell path and under the walnut tree and in through his own door. "It was my own fault," he said, as he opened the door. "I'll remember tomorrow, if I can."

He woke the next morning before it was light. He remembered what he must not do and was so afraid of swallowing even a drop of water that he did not go near the well. He went through the town before the light began to break. He didn't meet the milkman and he was glad of that: the milkman would have thought it very strange indeed if Falter Tom had refused to speak for a second time.

When he reached the point it was too dark for him to see the steps in the cliff and Falter Tom sat down, with his back against the old fig tree, and waited. He stared out to sea and watched the streaks of light spread in the sky. As soon as there was light enough he went down the steps to the beach. He was earlier than he had been yesterday; the beach was larger, though the tide was capturing it inch by inch. Falter Tom took off his old cap and polished its hard beak on his sleeve. He wanted to look his best for the water boy and the sea.

When the water boy called from the sea, Falter Tom was ready.

"I've done all you said," he called to the boy. "I've taken nothing to my lip for food or drink, and I've talked to no one, not even to myself, and that's a habit I have. And I'm not late, am I?"

"No, you're not," the boy said. He seemed very tired and his voice was hard to hear. "Part of a fish and a piece of gold, do you have that?"

"I have," Falter Tom said. "Do I put my foot in the sea?"

"No," the boy said. "There's no need, as long as you have done as I asked. You swear you have?"

"Aye, I swear."

"Then I believe you," the water boy said. "Now you have only to leave something behind, above high water, and walk out to me here. Leave your cap; that would do."

"Ah," Falter Tom said. "Must I leave that? I've had it so long."

The boy looked a long time at Falter Tom. "You have to give something up," he said patiently. "I've been half-way round the

world since yesterday morning's tide, just to make sure that you can come and that you'll be safe. You have to do something, too. Your cap would be the best thing to leave."

"Aye, aye," Falter Tom said, and put his cap down on a shelf of rock out of reach of the tide. "And now?"

"Take the charm and wrap it about your wrist. Will it go?"

"It will," Falter Tom said. "It has a clasp for that very job."

"Then come on," the boy cried happily, his voice suddenly stronger. "Come into the sea."

Falter Tom stepped bravely off the little island of sand over which the tide was rising and limped and faltered out into the water until he stood as he had done before up to his chin in the sea. It went well: he didn't feel either cold or wet. The sun was rising and the light struck into his eyes. "So far so good," he said. "Are you sure you can manage the rest of it? Old as I am, I'm too young for drowning."

"Trust me," the boy said. "We have the secret now. They have shown me what I must do."

31

"*They*, again?" Falter Tom said.

"Trust me," the water boy said once more.

"Well, I trust you, that's plain enough. Else I'd not be here. Let's get on then."

The water boy, his green body and shining hair catching the sun, put his cool smooth hand into the hand of Falter Tom. It was the first time Falter Tom had felt his touch.

"You must look at the track of the sun on the sea," the water boy said, slowly and clearly. "Look as long as you can until, when you close your eyes, there are gold coins falling under your lids. Then you must raise the charm on your wrist clear of the sea and with your eyes shut say these words: *Part of a fish and a piece of gold, kept all for luck; keep me lucky, now.* And at the last word you must lean back on the sea and sink down, without holding your breath. Without holding your breath, Falter Tom."

"I understand," Falter Tom said very quietly. "And if it doesn't work?"

"Why, you'll swallow a mouthful of sea-water and be none the worse. But if you will do as I say, it will work. I promise."

Falter Tom looked back to where he thought the black peak of his cap must be shining on the cliff, and turned again, and looked into the track of the sun on the sea. He stared without blinking for as long as he could, and when he could look no longer shut his eyes; and there, under the lids, were gold spots falling like dancing coins. He raised the charm clear of the water and slowly recited: "*Part of a fish and a piece of gold, kept all for luck; keep me lucky, now.*" He leaned back, and breathing steadily, though it was not easy to do, sank beneath the sea.

The water closed over him and there was nothing to mark his

32

going but one great gull that flew once over the ripples, called and cried, and flew on.

Falter Tom sank into the sea, breathing steadily, his eyes tightly closed. He bumped lightly on the sandy bottom, opened his eyes, and sat up. The first thing he saw was the water boy.

The boy's skin was different, the green darker, shot with flecks and speckles of colour, as beautiful as anything Falter Tom had ever seen. The boy's copper-coloured hair stirred in the water as he moved. He brought his strange handsome face very close to the whiskers of Falter Tom.

"There," the water boy said. "It's done. You are safe under the sea. Are you comfortable?"

Falter Tom nodded and began to speak: a cloud of bubbles burst from his mouth. He tried again and still couldn't get out a

33

word. The chain of bubbles rose above him. He was very puzzled.

"Don't worry," the water boy said. "I'll show you. You must say only one word with each breath to begin with. Say a word; say it softly."

"Hello," Falter Tom said, very carefully, and was pleased to hear his own voice again. A tiny string of bubbles went out with the word. "Hello," he said again.

"Splendid," the boy said. "In a moment you will have the trick of it. We must rest here a little while, until you get your sea-breath. There's no hurry. We have all the time in the world."

A cloud of bubbles rose from Falter Tom. The boy smiled and Falter Tom began again.

"It's more like a dream," Falter Tom said slowly. "My voice sounds different, quieter; and the sound of it doesn't carry."

"You can't speak loudly," the boy said. "There are no big voices in the sea. They say that if you try to shout the big bubbles take the word up to the surface, and when they break they let free a shout, on the sea top, where there are none to hear. Are you happy?"

"Perfectly," Falter Tom said. "Perfectly," he said again, and watched the bubbles rising. Would there be, he wondered, a

tiny echo of the word, muttering over the water when the
bubbles broke? CO. SCHOOLS C482945

"We must go before the tide turns," said the boy. "Low water
would uncover us here. Do you feel the stillness? It is dead water,
the moment between the tides. It will turn soon. There; do you
feel it? The tide is going back. We must go farther out. You'll
have to crouch a little at first or your head will poke out."

Falter Tom stood up, crouching, and walked after the green
boy. After a time he stood upright and strolled along, walking
on the sloping floor of the sea. Walking was easy, he found. He
said a few words to himself, to master the knack of it, then tried
a full sentence and a snatch of a song. The song drove the bubbles
up in hundreds. Falter Tom smiled; it was very amusing.

The water boy moved on, half swimming, half walking,
touching his toes lightly on the sea floor. Falter Tom copied him:
it was pleasant to do and not at all difficult; much as if he had
been walking on land, with a parachute on his back keeping him
almost clear of the ground. They walked so for a little while, and
then the water boy stopped and let himself sink until he was
sitting down. The sea bottom was no longer sandy, but rocky.

"We must find a place where we can rest," the water boy said.
"Until you are used to it all you mustn't do too much."

"I'm fine," Falter Tom said. "Never better."

"I must teach you to swim," the water boy said. "It's faster
than a sea-walk."

"Ah," Falter Tom said. "There's surely nothing in it if you
haven't the worry of keeping afloat."

He heaved himself forward and swam very slowly and very
clumsily around the boy, waving his arms and legs as though he
were a crazy windmill feeling the first touch of a fresh wind.

35

The water boy burst out laughing, apologized for being rude, and burst out laughing again. He was so amused that Falter Tom could hardly see him for bubbles.

"We could never get far like that," the water boy said. "This is what you do."

He shot away at a great speed, looking, Falter Tom thought, as though he had been fired from a cannon. His mane of hair streamed behind him. He swam, very fast, in a big loop through the sea, and came back. He circled very slowly around Falter Tom.

"Impossible," Falter Tom said. "I'll have to stick to my breast-stroke. That's not something I could manage at all."

"It's very easy," the water boy said. "If you'll only try. The way you do it is this. Imagine you are right up at the very top of the mast, on a ship, and want to dive into the sea."

"Lad," Falter Tom said, "there is nothing one would want less. 'Twould be a way of killing yourself, for sure."

"Yes, but just imagine," the water boy said. "Just pretend. How would you do it, then?"

"Why, I'd dive off," Falter Tom said. "Just fall."

"That's what you have to do, then," the water boy said. "You wouldn't try to breast-stroke your way down to the water, would you?"

"Indeed not," Falter Tom said. "It would look untidy, and queer."

"Then if you put your arms straight along your sides and keep your feet together, and keep your balance so that you don't tumble head over heels, you have only to fall through the sea. Up or down, or in whatever direction you like. You use your hands like fins, like a rudder. Do try."

Falter Tom and the Water Boy

Falter Tom tried: he kept his feet together and stretched his arms along his sides. He toppled slowly forward, smiling a little, and lay face down, stretched out very stiffly on the bed of the sea.

"You didn't push," the water boy said.

"I don't remember your mentioning it," Falter Tom said, in good humour. "Is it with my feet I'm to push? Or my hands?"

"With your head."

"Now swither me, boy," Falter Tom said. "Am I to stand on my head? A man of my age?"

"Please," the water boy said. "I'm serious. It's as if you tried to throw your head away and then dived after it with your body."

He showed Falter Tom what he meant and Falter Tom tried it. He kept on trying until he could glide forward, rather jerkily, quite a little distance. The boy clapped his hands in delight; it made no sound under the sea. Falter Tom tried again and again, and soon he was able to swim straight ahead, very smoothly and very fast. He was very proud of himself. He had a little trouble turning to come back and lost control and sank down through the sea like a leaf.

"That's where you use your hands," the water boy said, swimming up to him. "Follow me; you'll see then."

They glided off like strong, quick fish, and Falter Tom copied the water boy. They swam a long way, curving and turning, looping and sporting in the pale green light until Falter Tom had learned it all, the long rush, the sweeping turn, the climb, and the dive. Sometimes, however, starting off from the rocky sea floor, he forgot himself and tried to breast-stroke again, and until he remembered the boy's lesson he got nowhere at all. But soon he had the skill off to perfection. He was as proud as a boy who has learned to ride a bicycle, or a lively horse.

"It's wonderful," the boy said, his slanted eyes shining with delight. "You are very quick. It's because you know the sea. It's how fish swim: but you know that."

"Indeed, I didn't," Falter Tom said. "Though it's an excellent way of getting about. But now that you mention it I'd not look to see a snapper, say, doing the breast-stroke."

"Then if you're not too tired we will go somewhere where we can rest," the water boy said, and they swam off, side by side, out into the deeper water where the undersea light paled as they swam.

Falter Tom and the water boy swam for a long time: Falter Tom was surprised that he did not grow tired.

"It's growing darker," Falter Tom said to the water boy, as they swam side by side.

"We are swimming deep," the water boy said. "These are fishing grounds. You have to take care. The nets are dangerous."

"Aye," Falter Tom said. "I can well believe it. But how do you know where we are? How do you know we are going in the right direction? Could we not beach ourselves, by mistake?"

The water boy slowed down. "There are signs," he said. "Do you not feel the current? It streams past us like air. You can tell how deep you are by the feeling of tightness in your chest. We are almost there."

They began to rise up to where the light was stronger. Falter Tom felt the push of the current. The water boy stopped swimming and Falter Tom came up beside him; and then he found himself being forced slowly backward.

"Keep your head into it," the water boy said. "Lean against the stream. The merest flutter of your hand will hold you. There! you have it."

"It's pleasant," Falter Tom said. "It rests me."

"It's one of my favourite places," the water boy said. "I come here to sleep, sometimes. The water rocks me."

"Ah, you do sleep, then?" Falter Tom said. "It was a question that was puzzling me, I'll admit."

"This is to sleep," the water boy said. "The sleep of a fish. The water is warm and there is a soft light. Below us there is a darkness and the depths of the sea. And below that a great trench, a secret place which we can never explore. And yet we may go down quite deep, for all that."

"How deep, lad? As deep as whales dive?"

"No," the water boy said. "But I will show you the sea floor, and what no man's eyes have ever seen. You must take care to keep the charm tight on your wrist. If that is lost, you are lost too."

Falter Tom looked at the gold chain and whale-tooth charm; he tried the clasp and it was secure. "Are you not afraid of sharks?" he said. "Of killer whales and the giant octopus; and of the great squid I have read of but have never seen, though I have voyaged far enough and long enough to have seen most things. Are you not afraid of all these things?"

"I am never harmed," the water boy said. "There is an old peace between us, a sea-truce."

"A truce? I do not understand."

"An agreement," the boy said. "*They* have said it is to be so."

"They, boy?"

"The sea kings."

"Am I to see them, then?" Falter Tom asked.

"To hear them," the boy said. "They have something to say to you. We are going towards them."

They held themselves still and were gently rocked by the current, like trout in a river.

"Have you a name for me?" the boy asked. "You promised to find me one, Falter Tom. Do you remember?"

"Aye, I remember well enough. And I did think of one or two. But there are no nicknames, now."

"Why?" the boy asked. "What of your own?"

"It's a nickname no longer," Falter Tom said. "It no longer describes me, do you see? I can't be said to falter any more: I've lost my limp in the sea. I call you boy, or water boy, or my green lad, and they are name enough. They have a pleasant sound. We'll not interfere with that."

The water boy seemed pleased. He looked at Falter Tom and smiled; the points of his slanting eyes lifted merrily.

"But tell me, boy," Falter Tom said. "If you have never been out of the sea, how do you speak my tongue?"

"I am old," the water boy said. "I have had time to learn."

"Fifteen hundred and fifty; you are that old?" Falter Tom said, bubbling out a laugh at the joke.

"Older," the boy said. "I told you that, knowing that you would not believe me. Had I told you the truth, you might not have trusted me. I am, for all I know, as old as the sea. I can remember neither beginning nor growing. I have always been as I am now."

"Lad," Falter Tom said in wonder, "am I to believe you? It's not a thing I find easy to understand."

"I know your tongue," the boy said. "And others, too. I have lain at night on still water, by coracle and galleon, by trireme and slave ship. I have heard men talking, in all tongues, as they rested at night, chained to their oars. Men captured in sea fights and made to row an enemy ship—talking of home. I have lain as still as this, by fishermen's boats, keeping clear of the lights and the nets and the hooks, and I have heard their songs. I have swum alongside armed ships and heard sailors talk of war. I have lived so long that I know all the languages of the sea, of every country that touches on the ocean. Old languages, some of them, that I never hear now. But I have told you that. And ships I have seen that I never see now but on the sea bed wrecked and rotting."

"Are there others of you?" Falter Tom asked, rather nervously, amazed that a bit of a green lad, who looked no more than twelve, should be so old. "Have you a family, or anything like that? If I may ask?"

"The sea is large," the water boy said. "You will know that. I have not met with another like myself. I used to grow lonely sometimes, on calm nights in warm water. I would call to the ships, or rest beside them and sing to them. But they were frightened."

"Frightened?" Falter Tom said bravely. "Of a water boy? Surely not. There's no danger about you, is there?"

"They had no idea what I was," the boy said wisely. "I don't blame them. It's what you don't know that frightens you, I suppose."

"Aye," Falter Tom said. "But what do you live on, may I ask? What do you eat and drink? They are things I'd like to have the answer of; though I'd not like to be nosey, mind."

"Because of the truce," the boy said, "I may not eat anything in the sea. And I drink but rarely, at the sea-mouth of freshwater rivers. Long ago people used to leave offerings of food at the shore, and I fed well then, on strange sweetmeats and rare fruits. Now I eat but little, though the sea feeds all her tribe. But should you need food, *they* will provide it; whatever you wish."

"Swither me, boy," Falter Tom said in surprise. "Do you forget I'm used to three meals a day? All creatures need food, and I am no exception. I'd not like to face the thought of not eating again. There are things I've a tooth for: bacon and eggs; mushrooms fried in butter; home-made bread, and a good crisp apple."

"You forget that the chain is magic," the boy said. "Part of a fish and a piece of gold—you remember? It keeps you safe under the sea: it keeps you untroubled. There are no rules for you while you have that. You may do as you like. But we are rested now, and it is time to go."

"Now, what time ever would that be?" Falter Tom said, and reached for his watch. The current caught at his outstretched hand and spun him round like a catherine wheel; round and round until he felt quite giddy. He had to think carefully before he could remember how to right himself, and just for a moment he was about to begin his breast-stroke again; but he stopped himself in time and swam as the boy had taught him. When he was alongside the water boy again he took out his watch, very carefully, leaned a little to one side, and looked at it.

"That's no use," the water boy said, laughing so that a string of bubbles, like clear glass beads, hung above him a moment and were whisked away. "That sort of time has no meaning, under the sea. There is no night, unless we choose to lie in darkness. We swim fast enough to follow the sun as it shines on the sea."

Falter Tom held the watch tight against his side and thought about there being no clock-time under the sea. He thought about there being no night and no day except what they chose for themselves, light water or dark. It was a thought very difficult for him to understand.

"I'll make you a present, then," Falter Tom said, and, holding himself steady by one fluttering hand, held out the watch to the boy. "I'll give you this as a toy. 'Tis a good watch and keeps faithful time."

The water boy shook his head. "Thank you," he said, "but what would I do with it? I've nowhere to put it. I've no pockets."

"Ah, forgive me," Falter Tom said. "I was forgetting that. And you're somewhat old for toys, I daresay. I've my jacket and britches still, and pockets enough. What, by the way, will become of them, my clothes and my boots, in the sea like this?"

"That depends on what you decide when you hear what they've got to say to you. At present you're on holiday, under the sea, and your clothes won't come to any more harm than they would on any other holiday. They won't get dirty."

The water boy was pleased at his little joke.

"Do we go to them, now?" Falter Tom asked. "Whoever they are. Kings, was it, you called them?"

"The sea kings," the boy said softly. "They live in the Great Sea Cave and their voices rule the sea. No one has ever seen them as they are. They disguise themselves as fish, or as giant gulls. The sea is their kingdom. We are going towards them. Are you rested?"

"Aye, I am. Quite, quite rested."

"Then we will go on," the water boy said.

They moved together, the man and the boy, gliding easily across the current. The water boy chose the direction and they swam on, fast and cool and safe in the sea.

Falter Tom and the Water Boy

The sea was rich: in the calm depths there was a wealth of wonder, and Falter Tom, swimming hard on the green heels of the water boy, saw much to surprise and delight him.

They swam, by roundabout ways, towards the Cave of the Voices.

They swam slower in the deep water and the boy's green skin gave off a shining, milky glow, so that Falter Tom had no diffi-

culty in following him. They swam over ancient wrecks where only the most frail skeleton marked the outline of a ship. They looked into the worn, drowned faces of old figureheads that waited only a touch, a slight eddy of water, to collapse into a shapeless mound. Falter Tom swam under the high and towering poops of vessels strangely preserved by some trick of the sea, the carving and decoration still clear to his curious sailor's eye. Once they saw a heavy cabin door swing at some movement of the water as they passed, as if inviting them in; but the sea, needing no such invitation, was there before them, making itself at home in the cabin. There were ancient ships of a kind Falter Tom had never seen, with a rack of decks like the trays in a baker's oven; long beak-prowed ships, pierced for oars; fast sailing ships and rusting tramp steamers, all at rest, decaying in the sea. Many

would have crumbled to nothing long since except that the sand had preserved them, piling above them for hundreds of years, and then washing away again. Many lay even yet under their gravemounds of sand and Falter Tom could only wonder what lay beneath; though sometimes the water boy could tell him what was there, having seen them before they were covered.

What cargoes they had carried Falter Tom could only guess:

gold, silver, spices, rusting iron. The tea ships, he thought, must have gone down like giant teapots, their holds, for a little while, filled with a strange and cold brew of salty tea, as the chests broke and the tea leaves spilled out.

Crusts of sea creatures were fastened upon the sunken ships; sea gardens of pale plants grew upon them; starfish lay on the decks and sea-snails crawled slowly over the broken rigging where once, furling sails, active sailors had climbed. Falter Tom found he could poke his finger through steel hulls, that deck rails and stanchions crumbled away at his touch like melting candy floss. Bright fish hunted through cabins that had once held who knows what proud passenger or captain.

At one such wreck, lying in shallower water where it was quite light, Falter Tom and the water boy swam right through the ghostly cabins. They were careful not to tread upon the sloping deck or to touch the ship in any way. It was a very old wreck. They swam through the broken hull into the hold, and the sight that met their eyes made Falter Tom gasp. There, dull and ancient coins spilled from rotting chests and lay in heaps upon the sea floor. Bars of gold lay about, like logs of firewood ready for anyone's gathering. The water boy could not understand Falter Tom's excitement.

"But, boy," Falter Tom said, "do you not see? It's gold. Enough to buy an empire. It was likely some ship homeward bound from El Dorado."

"Where's that?" the boy asked.

"Nowhere," Falter Tom said. "It doesn't exist. Though the Spaniards searched for it, so I've read—the City of Gold. But when I look at this, a mountain of treasure, it seems they might have found it, even so."

"It's no use," the water boy said. "It's too heavy; and it doesn't stay bright."

They rested in the water, just under the leaning hull. Falter Tom counted the gold bars lying on the sea floor: there were hundreds. He gave a great shout of excitement, and a very curious thing happened. There was, as usual, no sound of shouting, only a rush of bubbles, but the wrecked ship began to tremble. The deck and hull, the bridge and the bow and the high stern shivered like a shadow on water, shaken by the silent echo of his shout; and the whole delicate husk of the once solid treasure ship floated gently down, a haze of tiny, separate grains, drifting and falling to the sea bed. Falter Tom was amazed and a little afraid. He turned quickly to swim away and scraped over the strewn gold bars. It was a light blow and he scarcely felt it; but when he looked at his wrist the chain and the whale-tooth charm were gone. Falter Tom held out his bare arm to the water boy. At the same moment he began to find it difficult to breathe. His eyes hurt, and he seemed to be lying in darkness with a great weight on his chest. He was very frightened now.

"Quick," the water boy said, putting his mouth right up against Falter Tom's ear. "Quick, or you are lost. Grasp my ankles, and hold on very tight. We must get to the sea top and the air."

Falter Tom caught hold and the water boy shot upwards, towing him out of the depths, swimming so fast that Falter Tom's hair and whiskers were pressed flat against his skin and each hair hurt separately, as though it were being plucked out. They went up so fast that the water boy dived clear of the water, like a leaping fish, and Falter Tom, letting go his grip, fell with a great belly-buster splash, back into the sea. He gasped, winded by the blow, and began to tread water to keep himself afloat. The water boy swam back to him; his handsome face was frowning.

"It's very bad," the water boy said. "Unless I can find the charm again, you are lost. Without it you can do nothing. You cannot breathe or swim under the sea. You can only tread water here until you can keep afloat no longer, and then you will drown. You have lost your magic, all that kept you safe in the sea."

"Lad," Falter Tom said, puffing and blowing; "you've no need to tell me that. I'm in a fix and I know it. I don't wish to join the gold bars on the bottom. I wish I'd never seen them. 'Twas likely a gold bar I struck with my wrist, do you see?"

"Put your arm about my shoulder," the water boy said. "I will hold you. There. Now we have just one chance. About a sea league from here, towards the sun's rising, there is a rock in the sea. The rock on which the treasure ship struck. I will take you there and return, alone, and search for the charm. The rock is bare and the sea will sweep you off if this wind rises; but it is the only chance we have. Take hold of my ankles again, shut your eyes against the water, and we will go. We haven't much time."

The water boy towed Falter Tom through the sea. They had to rest often because Falter Tom, having lost his sea-breath, kept swallowing mouthfuls of water. They reached the rock. The sea swelled about it but Falter Tom managed to climb to a high point where, on a narrow ledge, he crouched down. The water boy waved, dived and was gone.

Falter Tom felt lonely and cramped and cold: once the charm had left his wrist he had been soaked to the skin by the sea. He took off his jacket, moving very carefully on the rocky shelf, and wrung it out. He wrapped it about him again and stared at the sea. In the middle of the vast ocean he was quite alone. He began to wish for his cabin cottage; for the white shell path and the walnut tree; for the bright oil lamp and the fire over which he could boil a kettle for tea. How long, he wondered, had he been away from it all? What would they make of his going off like that, without a word, and leaving his cap on the beach?

He had very little hope of the water boy's finding the charm. How could you find anything in an ocean as vast as this? And yet the boy knew his way about in the sea. Falter Tom looked at the sun shining in a clear sky. If it weren't for the wind, he thought, I'd be warmer. By the look of the sun it is after noon. There are some hours yet to nightfall. And then? Ah well, he sighed, there have been sailors drowned before, and should I fall asleep and

49

nod into the sea, or die from hunger and cold, I'll need no bit of
a charm then to keep me in the sea. My white old bones will lie
among gold coins; I'll rest among bullion; and I'll have come to
grief, for sure.

It was just before nightfall, between the sunset and the coming
of dark, when the water boy returned to the rock. Falter Tom
had wedged himself tight on his ledge and had fallen stiffly asleep.
It was a trick he had learned in his sailoring days: he could sleep
sound on the top strand of a barbed-wire fence, he used to
boast. And he slept now. Above his head a giant gull perched on
the very peak of the rock; but Falter Tom did not know it. The
gull flew down to the water boy and they seemed to talk together,
rising and falling in the swell of the sea about the lonely rock.
The gull was careful to keep beak-on into the wind: ruffled
feathers were painful. In a little while the gull flew off, beating
once past Falter Tom's face to wake him.

"Falter Tom, Falter Tom," the water boy cried. "I have it.
It's here. Climb down."

Falter Tom was stiff and cold. He couldn't remember where
he was. He had dreamed that he was washing himself in icy water
from the well at the back of his cottage. In the west a last glare of
sunset met his eye. He looked down from his rock.

"I was preparing to die," he said.

"I lifted every bar of gold in the wreck, I think," the water
boy said. "The charm was hidden under the last."

"It's ever that way," Falter Tom said. "You have it then? I
am safe?"

"Safe," the boy cried. "But now, before you enter the water,
you must leave something behind again. What will it be?"

Falter Tom and the Water Boy

Falter Tom patted his pockets, took out the watch and laid it on the ledge. "There, lad," he said. "Will that do? I'm forever leaving bits of myself here and there, it seems. But I don't complain. It's no time for talking. I'm apt to freeze to death in this wind; and my teeth chatter together with a noise like ice in a tumbler. I feel I'll never be warm again."

"Fix this on," the boy said. "Tightly." And he passed up the charm. "And now, come into the sea."

"Is it the words and all I've to say again?" Falter Tom asked, taking a faltering step off the rock.

"Breathe and sink," the water boy said. "But be quick. I will take you to warm water to drive off your chill."

Falter Tom sank into the sea, and in just a few minutes, remembering the trick of it, he was following the water boy, swimming underwater as fast as he could, though he felt his muscles aching a little from the cold. The water boy was leading him to sandy shallows where the sun warmed the clear water; to a place where he could lie and soak the heat slowly into his bones.

"All we ever found of him was the cap," the postmaster said to the visiting lawyer. "Out at the point there, at the tip of the bay. He was there a lot, in all sorts of weather, to watch the sea. A pleasant manner of man he was; called Falter for his limp, you know. Maybe a mite queer a week or so before he lost himself; not talking to the milkman, and asking me foolish riddles, and things like that. Yes, queer. But only a trifle, you understand. Seventy-one years old, he was. I guessed it to the very year; what do you think of that?"

"Drowned, you say?" the lawyer said.

"Ah, now, we don't know that," the postmaster said. "Gone, yes; but a man's hat doesn't tell tales. We miss him, of course. A sort of town character, you know?"

"And his house? What of that?" the lawyer asked.

"Closed up," the postmaster said. "It's down the street a way. You can't miss it. A sort of cabin cottage, with a white shell path and a walnut tree; and a well at the back. We dare not touch it for fear he should come faltering back one day, and want it. He's been gone about a year, I'd say."

"A pity," the lawyer said. "I'd some money for him, you see. Yes. Quite a lot, in fact. A great deal of money, you might say. Yes. A *very* great deal of money. A fortune. Yes. Left him by a shipmate, it was. However, money isn't like apples is it? It won't go bad with keeping—ha ha. Still, I'll inquire for him again in a year or two. Meantime, good-bye. Pleasant little town you have here, by the way. Sleepy, of course, after the city. Nothing much happens, I suppose? The tide comes in and goes out, eh? Yes. Well, good-bye again."

"I've forgotten the riddle," the postmaster said to the lawyer's back. "No time for puzzles, you know. Still he may turn up. It

52

will be good news for him, though you haven't much use for a *lot* of money at seventy-one, I suppose. Or seventy-two he'd be now. But I'll give him your card if I see him. Good-bye."

The water boy brought Falter Tom at last to the Cave of the Voices, to the home of the sea kings whose voices ruled the sea. The cave was fathoms deep. Falter Tom and the water boy swam close. A shining weed, brighter than the boy's body, grew over the entrance, and a giant shark glided slowly back and forth.

"Don't be afraid," the water boy said. "Stand here, quite still, and you will come to no harm. I will announce you."

The water boy swam through the glowing curtain. Falter Tom stood quite still and waited, keeping one eye on the shark. He even tried a smile and a nod, but the shark's expression did not change. From the cave there came a murmuring sound, like surf on a distant beach, or like the sound of the sea locked in a hollow shell. The weeds stirred gently as the shark swam past, and stirred again as the water boy came through. He took Falter Tom by the hand and led him up to a rock shaped like a rough table with a flat top.

"Stand here," the water boy said. "Do as the voices direct you; and do not be afraid. They intend you no harm."

Falter Tom stood alone by the rock. The surging sound within the cave grew louder, and suddenly he was listening to a voice that was like no other voice he had ever heard, round and hollow and booming, a sound like five or six voices speaking exactly together.

"Falter Tom," the voices said. "Lay down the charm upon the rock, and hear what we have to say."

Falter Tom looked through the weird light, caught the water

boy's nod, and placed the chain on the rock.

"Falter Tom. The time has come when you must decide. Your holiday in the sea is done. Now you must choose, either to remain in the sea, for ever, or to go from it, for ever. Wait. Do not stir yet. Listen close. These are the conditions.

"Should you choose to remain in the sea you must give up the charm, and be ruled by us, who rule the sea. In return, we will make you this gift: you shall be safe, unharmed by sea creatures or the salt sea itself, and you shall never be older than you are at this moment. You may not, then, ever leave the sea, for should you put both feet together on dry land you will die as fish die, gasping for the sea. Keep that rule and we will keep you safe, to do what you will in the sea, to explore its wonders, learn its languages, see its vast sea sights.

"Should you decide to return to land the water boy will take you to your own bay and you will find yourself, seated under the old fig tree that grows on the point, and waking as though from a long sleep. You will have no memory of this sea-change, no memory of the water boy, nor of any of the things you have seen and done. The charm will be in your pocket but its magic will have gone. You will have no answer to the question of where you have been.

"That is the choice. You have the time of three tides in which to consider it. Meantime the charm must lie on the rock. Go now, and return with your answer."

The sea voices rolled back into the cave and died away to a light lapping whisper. The shark kept up its slow and dangerous glide. Falter Tom walked lightly up to the water boy, and without speaking they swam off, rising towards the light and the warm water.

55

"Can you guess how long, in land time, you have been in the sea?" the water boy asked.

"Some days," Falter Tom said. "A week or so. I haven't the exact reckoning."

They were basking in warm water, just under the skin of the sea, much as though they had been floating just under a jade-green and brilliant ceiling.

"One year of land time," the water boy said. "That is how long. And on the land they have forgotten you. They think you are drowned."

"Ah, lad, I know not how to deal with all this," Falter Tom said. "I've not the head for such heavy questions. What shall I do?"

"Stay," the water boy said softly. "There's a world we can enjoy, in the sea. You have not touched on the fringe of its wonders."

"Is it as easy, boy, as you say? I've lived my life on land, on the surface of the sea, in air, these seventy-odd years. I have the habit of it now. It wouldn't be easy to give up."

"No," the water boy said. "And yet you heard the voices. Your sea-life is just beginning; you have all time before you. On land, you are close to death. Three score years and ten are behind you."

"Aye, lad," Falter Tom said, gazing up at the fast flickering reflection of the sun on the sea. "But then I've no great fear of death. I've lived a life. And I have, too, a taste for human company; though I mean no unkindness in saying that."

"But we may touch on land," the water boy said. "You may look on the shore; even on the lights of your town. You may lie in the sea shallows and listen to the voices of men, and all the

tongues of the sea. And you will never be older than you are now."

"It's not easy," Falter Tom said, and rubbed at his white trim whiskers that in a year had never grown awry. "It's not easy and there's so little time."

"I will take you down," the water boy said. "To a quiet place. And you must make up your mind, alone. When three tides have risen and fallen, I will come for you, and take you to the cave. You must have your answer ready."

They turned, rolled over like dolphins, and dived. The water boy led Falter Tom to a tiny white coral cave where the water was not quite deep enough to shut out all the light. They touched hands, rather sadly, and the water boy, green still and only faintly gleaming, flecks of colour lighting his face and running in the long mane of his hair, swam very slowly away.

Falter Tom sat down alone to think. He reached for his pipe and then remembered that it would not light in the sea. He remembered too that he had not smoked for a year. He sighed to himself. It was all too difficult, too difficult.

There was the water boy to think of, of course. He couldn't easily face the thought of not seeing him ever again. And the boy was right of course. He, Falter Tom, had lived his full land-life nearly through; he would return to the town only to grow older and quietly die. Here, under the sea, with all the freedom of the fastest fish, he could live on, explore and gaze upon wonders enough for a dozen life-times. All true; all true, he thought. But once I have chosen, either way, there is no way back. And then, the water boy saved my life: we have not spoken of it, but it must be considered. Perhaps, if he saved it, it is his. But no, the lad would have no such thought.

He sat on, wondering, trying to find an answer. He tried to balance one thought against another; it was, really, too difficult.

He fell into a doze, the sleep of a fish, his eyes open and his body pillowed by the sea.

"How well I've learned to speak and swim," he muttered sleepily to himself. "How well. And as for the other—why, we'll look into that when the time comes."

When the time came the water boy woke Falter Tom out of his long sea-nap and together, without speaking, they swam to the Cave of the Voices. Falter Tom took up his place at the flat rock and looked at the shining weed curtain once more, at the charm which lay upon the rock, at the shark slowly swimming. The cave began to boom with sound.

"Have you your answer, Falter Tom?" the great voices chanted. "If you would return to the land, take up your charm, and go. If you would stay in the sea, take up the charm and throw it into the mouth of the cave. We wait."

Falter Tom took up the charm. He looked back through the weak light to where the water boy, shining, as milky and as soft as a pearl, watched him solemnly, frowning with his slanting eyes. He held the chain in his hand and stepped clear of the rock. The shark moved off to a distance and held itself still in the sea.

Falter Tom looked at the cave again, at the shark, at the water boy. He was making up his mind. His next step would decide his future; forward for the sea, backward for the land. He raised his foot. The water boy swam a little closer and Falter Tom looked towards the movement: the water boy was between him and the mouth of the cave. The water boy was smiling.

"Is it a time for smiles, lad?" Falter Tom said, so softly that there were hardly any bubbles at all. He kept his foot raised. "Is it a time for smiles, do you think?"

"Yes," the boy said in his familiar, light and piping voice. "Yes, I feel it is."

"Then look," Falter Tom said. "Look."

He let the charm hang down and, with his fingers, gently twirled it, around and around. The water boy stood on tiptoe, delicate and handsome and green, watching and smiling. Without sign of a falter, Falter Tom crossed the sea floor, under the long nose of the guarding shark, and dropped the charm, the gold chain and the white whale-tooth, into the mouth of the murmuring cave.

The water boy's shout of joy started so many bubbles that the shark shied nervously away. When it swam back again Falter Tom and the water boy had gone. They had gone without trace as though they had never been.